Stilesville Starz

by Christine Peymani

Angelika

D1465072

Bath · New York · Singapore · Hong Kong · Cologne · Delhi · Melbourne

First published by Parragon in 2007
Parragon
Queen Street House
4 Queen Street
Bath BA1 1HE, UK

ISBN 978-1-4054-9962-0

Printed in the UK

Chapter One

"I can't believe we only have three weeks of summer left!" Sasha exclaimed. She and her best friends Cloe, Jade and Yasmin had just started their back-to-school shopping – they needed totally fresh looks for the new school year.

"I love shopping with a purpose," Jade declared. "And getting cute clothes to start the school year right is the best purpose of all!"

"I think we're doing pretty well so far," Yasmin pointed out, gesturing towards the many shopping bags each of her friends was lugging around.

"Hey, you guys, what's going on out there?" Cloe interrupted, looking out of the floor-to-ceiling windows in the mall's atrium to the town square below.

Her friends ran to her side and crowded against the glass. "It looks like they're setting up to shoot a movie," Sasha announced, peering down at the crew members, video cameras, lights and sound equipment crowding the streets.

"Whoa, how long were we shopping?" Jade wondered. "It looks like a movie crew has taken over our entire town while we've been in here."

"Oh my gosh, I think you're right!" Cloe squealed. "We'd better get down there!"

With that, she raced out of the mall with her best friends trailing behind her.

"Whoa," she sighed once they were in the middle of the square, surrounded by dozens of people hard at work turning their little town into a movie set. "It's amazing! But what would a movie crew be doing in Stilesville?"

"Besides shooting a movie, you mean?" Jade teased.

"Why would anyone shoot a movie in Stilesville?" Cloe asked. Her friends stared at her and she hurriedly added, "I mean, I love Stilesville, but it doesn't exactly seem like Hollywood material."

"Sure it does," Yasmin protested. "It's

pretty, it's got lots of cool locations…"

"And the locals aren't bad either," interrupted a tall, slender blonde guy, strolling up to join the girls.

"Um, thanks," Cloe replied, rolling her eyes at her friends. But then she turned to see who had spoken and gasped. "Oh my gosh, Devin DeVivo! You're, like, my all-time favourite actor. What are you doing here?"

"Starring in my next movie," he replied, shooting her a charming smile. "And looking for my next co-star, of course."

"What do you mean?" Sasha interrupted.

"Since we're shooting on location, we wanted to amp up the local flavour by casting some local talent," explained a man in a sports jacket and sunglasses, ambling over to join the girls. He swept one hand through his dark, curly hair, then held his hand out to Cloe. "Jake Austin," he said, shaking her hand.

"Jake Austin, the director?" Jade cried, nudging Cloe aside so she could take the man's hand instead. "I love your movies," Jade gushed.

"That's always good to hear," Jake said, smiling.

"Oh wow, is that Lexy MacAdams?" Yasmin interrupted, gazing across the square at a tall, willowy woman who was peering at a script.

"It sure is," Jake replied. "Would you like to meet her?"

"Would I ever!" Yasmin gasped. "She's, like, the coolest screenwriter ever! I just wish I could write like her!"

"Yasmin's just being modest," Sasha announced. "She's a fabulous writer."

"Hey, Lexy, over here!" Jake shouted, waving the screenwriter over.

"I'll have the rewrite for you in a minute," Lexy murmured, looking frenzied as she brushed her wavy golden hair back from her face.

"It's not that, Lex," Jake told her. "I just wanted you to meet your biggest fan."

Lexy looked up from her script for the first time and noticed Yasmin grinning goofily at her.

"Would you – um – would you sign my notebook?" Yasmin asked, dropping her shopping bags and rummaging in her bag for her reporter's notebook.

"I'd be happy to," Lexy agreed, flashing Yasmin a wide smile.

"It is such an honour to meet you!" Yasmin squealed while Lexy scrawled her signature. "You're my all-time favourite writer. I want to be just like you!"

"Where's that rewrite?" called a stocky, bearded man with a British accent.

"Oops, duty calls," Lexy said, handing Yasmin's notebook back to her. "Great meeting you!"

She rushed off, with Jake and Devin following behind.

"Who was that guy?" Yasmin asked.

"Only Ian Erickson, the most powerful producer in Hollywood," Sasha told her friends.

"How'd you recognize him?" Yasmin wanted to know.

"I like to keep tabs on all of the Hollywood movers and shakers," Sasha explained. "I figure it'll come in handy when I'm one of them someday."

"Well, at least you aim small," Jade teased.

"Of course I don't," Sasha declared. "If

you aim small, you'll be small and that is totally not my style!"

"The girl has a point," Jade agreed. "So, Yas, what did Lexy write to you?"

"'From one writer to another, good luck,'" Yasmin read. "See, I told you she was the coolest!" She clutched her notebook to her chest happily.

"That's awesome," Cloe said. "So, how are we going to get ourselves into her latest, greatest movie?"

"Besides auditioning like everyone else, you mean?" Yasmin teased.

"Obviously," Cloe replied with a grin.

"Okay then, I have a plan to get us on to the inside track," Sasha announced. She grabbed the arm of a skinny young crew member who was walking by and asked, "Can you tell me where the production office is?"

"Over there," he replied, pointing towards a long trailer at the edge of the square before rushing off among the tangle of cords and piles of equipment.

"Come on, girls," Sasha said. "We've got work to do!"

The girls marched over to the trailer and burst through the door. A girl with short black hair who looked only a little older than the four friends sat behind a desk, busily answering phones and typing away on her computer. She glanced up at the girls and held up one finger to tell them to wait.

The girls looked around the tiny office, crowded with scripts and after a moment the young woman behind the desk called, "Can I help you ladies?"

"We were wondering if you could use any production assistants," Sasha explained.

"I could," the girl began cautiously. "Have you ever worked on a movie before?"

"No," Sasha admitted. "But we learn fast and we work hard. Try us out for a couple of days and you'll see for yourself."

"I do need more local crew members," the girl said. "You're all from Stilesville?"

"Born and raised," Jade agreed.

The girl stared at them for a moment, then nodded. "We'll give it a try. You can start tomorrow, but for now, take this paperwork and a copy of the script home so you can get up to speed. Report to me at seven a.m. And wear comfortable shoes – you'll be doing a lot of running around." She handed them a pile of papers and the girls exchanged grins.

"You won't regret it!" Cloe squealed.

As they headed for the door, their new boss added, "I'm Melanie, by the way."

"Thanks, Melanie!" the girls chorused as they hurried out of the trailer.

Outside, the girls all paused and looked at Sasha. "So it's exciting to be working on a movie, but how exactly is that going to help us get cast in the movie?" Jade asked.

"First of all, we have the script, which none of the other actresses would, right?" Sasha explained. As her friends nodded, she continued, "And we'll be working every day with the people who make all the decisions, so that

©MGA

can't hurt either, right?" Her friends nodded again. "So I'd say it's a pretty good plan, right?"

"Yes, Sasha, as always, you're right!" Yasmin teased.

"That's what I like to hear," Sasha said, laughing.

"Now that that's taken care of, can we get back to my place?" Jade asked. "Because I'm still eager to see the new outfits that everyone bought today. Aren't you, guys?"

"Totally!" the girls agreed.

Chapter Two

"That is the cutest back-to-school look ever!" Jade exclaimed, checking out the ruffled skirt and tank top that Yasmin had picked out for the first day of school.

Yasmin did a little twirl, then collapsed on Jade's bed beside her friends. "I can't wait to show it off on the first day of school. You guys really like it?"

"Love it," Cloe agreed. "But we have a different big first day tomorrow – shouldn't we be prepping for that first? I mean, I have no idea what to wear on set!"

"I'm wearing capris, a baby tee and sneakers," Jade replied. "I think that'll make a good production assistant uniform."

"Sounds good to me," Sasha said. "But more importantly, we need to get this script read."

"Then let's get started!" Yasmin darted into the bathroom to change out of her new outfit, then grabbed a script and a spot on the floor. The girls read quickly and when they had finished, they looked at each other in excitement.

"This script is amazing!" Cloe cried. "We're gonna have the best time being in this movie together!"

"Well, I don't know if that's exactly possible," Sasha told her friends.

"Sasha, what happened to thinking big?" Yasmin protested.

"It's just, they have the cast list right here and it looks like the only role they haven't cast yet is the lead girl, Sophie Grace," Sasha explained. "I don't think we can all play her."

"Hmm, you're probably right," Jade agreed. "So what do we do?"

"I don't want to compete against you guys!" Yasmin interjected.

"Well then, I have the perfect solution," Cloe announced. "I'll go for the part and you'll all help me get it."

"Wait a second," Sasha protested. "Why should you be the only one who gets to audition?"

"Because I'm the one who wants to be an actress!" Cloe cried. "And I'm always the star in our school plays, so don't you think I have the best shot?"

"That's not fair, Cloe," Jade complained.

"Look, you girls have your talents too," Cloe replied. "But acting just happens to be mine."

"I guess we'll just have to see how the auditions go, then," Sasha told her, "because I'm definitely trying out."

"What for? You don't even care about acting," Cloe declared.

"That's not true," Sasha said. "But even more than acting, I care about getting to know Ian Erickson. I think I'd make a great Hollywood producer someday and snagging this part is the best way I can think of to get the attention of an important guy like him."

"I'm trying out too," Jade chimed in. "What could be cooler than being directed by the most talented director in the world?"

Yasmin sat silently flipping through her copy of the script and Cloe turned to her eagerly. "At least you're standing by me, right Yas?" Cloe asked.

"Of course I'll support you," Yasmin

began slowly, "but I think I have to take my shot too. It's a great opportunity to work closely with Lexy and I can't pass that up. I mean, she's totally my writing idol!"

"But wouldn't you rather work with her behind the scenes?" Cloe suggested.

"Sasha's right that we're more likely to get noticed as stars than as production assistants," Yasmin replied. "So I think I have to shoot for the spotlight, just this once."

Cloe crossed her arms over her chest, sulking.

"Come on, Cloe, don't be like that," Jade pleaded with her friend.

"You know, I should probably get going," Cloe muttered. "We've got a big day tomorrow and I'm really tired."

"But don't you think we should start rehearsing?" Sasha suggested. "I mean, the whole point of getting the script today was to get a jump on our competition."

"Maybe you haven't put it together yet, but you guys are my competition," Cloe snapped. "Even though you were supposed to be my friends." With that, Cloe grabbed her shopping bags and ran for the front door without a backward glance at the other girls.

"Wow, I don't think I've ever seen Cloe that angry," Yasmin murmured once the door had closed behind their friend.

"You know our Cloe," Sasha replied. "She's always getting all worked up about something, but she always calms down again."

"I don't know – she seemed really upset this time," Yasmin replied. "And she does kind of have a point."

Her friends stared at her and Yasmin continued in a rush, "I mean, we all want the part because it could help us do something else. But acting is the thing Cloe wants to do, so maybe it does make more sense for her to get the part."

"Acting is one of the things Cloe wants to do," Sasha pointed out. "Along with being an artist, or a football star or a filmmaker. It's not like she's exactly devoted her life to acting."

"But Sasha, we're still in high school," Yasmin interrupted. "It's not like any of us have devoted our lives to anything yet!"

"Look, just don't let Cloe guilt trip you into giving up something you really want," Jade chimed in. "It would be an amazing opportunity for any one of us, so we just have to take our shot and see what happens."

"And whoever gets the part can help hook the others up with the cool contacts they need," Sasha added.

"That's true..." Yasmin looked up at her friends and smiled. "And Cloe will see that too, right?"

"Eventually," Jade promised. "We just have to give her some time to cool down a little."

*   *   *

But Cloe was in her own bedroom, not cooling down at all. "How can they do this to me? They're totally destroying my

20

dream!" she ranted, stomping around her room until her mum, Katie, rapped lightly on her door.

"Cloe, did something happen at the mall?" Katie asked.

"Not at the mall – outside of the mall," Cloe replied, still pacing.

"Do you want to tell me about it?" Katie urged, sitting down on the edge of her daughter's bed.

Cloe whirled to face her mum and demanded, "Did you know there's a movie crew in town?"

"I might have heard something about that," Katie agreed, her eyes twinkling. "Actually, I'm providing their on-set catering!"

"Mum, that's awesome!" Cloe cried, forgetting for a moment that she was upset. "That's a huge job for you!"

"I know!" Katie exclaimed. "And if you help me, I can get you on the set."

"Actually mum, we got jobs today as production assistants," Cloe told her mum. "So I'll already be on set doing that."

"How exciting!" Katie squealed. "My little girl, working on a major Hollywood movie! So then, what are you so upset about?"

"I want to do more than work on the movie," Cloe explained, sitting down next to her mum. "They want to cast someone from Stilesville and I'm going for the part."

"Sweetheart, that's great," Katie told her.

"Yeah, but my friends are all auditioning too!" Cloe blurted out. "It's so unfair! They don't even want to act, but they refuse to back off and just support me!"

"But honey, if they want to audition, don't you think you should support them too?" Katie suggested.

"Acting is my dream!" Cloe protested. "They can't just take it from me!"

"That's right, they can't," Katie agreed. "If you work hard for this part, I'm sure you can earn it. But you can't expect your friends to just hand it to you."

"Of course not!" Cloe replied. "I mean, they couldn't anyway. Even if they weren't going for it, I'd still have to beat other girls for the part." She flopped dramatically back onto her bed and heaved a huge sigh. "I just didn't want to have to compete against my best friends, you know?"

"It doesn't really have to be a competition, you know," Katie pointed out. "Why can't you all help each other and be happy for whoever gets the part?"

"But if we all want it, how can we be happy for someone who beats us?" Cloe demanded.

"Because you're best friends," Katie explained. "And that's what best friends do."

Cloe sat up and gave her mum a hug. "You always make me feel better," she announced.

"That's what mums do," Katie said, hugging her daughter back.

Chapter Three

Early the next morning, before her alarm could even go off, Cloe's phone rang, waking her up.

"Hello?" she muttered groggily, struggling to sit up.

"Cloe, it's Yasmin," her friend said, sounding surprisingly cheerful. "Sorry to call you so early, but I just heard from Melanie and they want us on set right away. So I wanted to see if you wanted a lift."

"Oh – um – sure," Cloe agreed uncertainly. She glanced at her clock and saw that it was six a.m. – way too early to be up during the summer. She still hadn't decided if she was ready to make up with her friends, but she was too tired to argue.

"Great!" Yasmin exclaimed. "We'll be there in 20 minutes! Bye!" With that, she hung up before Cloe could say another word.

Cloe climbed slowly out of bed. "How am I supposed to make myself look presentable in 20 minutes?" she grumbled. She headed for the bathroom and spotted her mum already in the kitchen, busily preparing food for the movie's cast and crew.

"Isn't it a little early to be cooking?" Cloe asked.

"Nope!" her mum replied. "I've had doughnuts and bagels delivered already, but they're

©MGA

expecting a full breakfast by eight and I still have a lot of work to do!"

"Mum, how can you be such a morning person, when I am so totally not?" Cloe wondered.

"Maybe you'll grow up to be a morning person like me," Katie suggested.

"Ugh!" Cloe groaned. "That does not sound like something to look forward to!"

Her mum just laughed as Cloe wandered into the bathroom and climbed into the shower.

By the time she got out, she finally felt awake and ready to face the day. She threw on her robe and dashed back to her bedroom, where she stared in despair at her wardrobe. "I don't have anything to wear!" she complained. But then she spotted her shopping bags from the day before and smiled.

She rummaged around in them and pulled out a pair of khaki capris and a fluttery-sleeved top. "I was saving you for school, but I think showing you off on the set will work too," she told the clothes. She quickly got dressed, then admired herself in her full-length mirror. "Do I look like star material, or what?"

"Cloe, your friends are here!" Katie called from the kitchen. Cloe hurriedly ran a brush through her hair and smoothed on some lip-gloss, then darted into the living room.

"Good morning, ladies!" she exclaimed when she saw her friends waiting by the front door. "Are you ready to show those Hollywood honchos who's boss?"

"Um, sure," Jade replied, shooting her friends a confused glance. She'd expected Cloe to still be sulking, but she seemed totally upbeat.

28

"Bye, girls!" Katie called as the four best friends scurried out of the door. "Maybe I'll see you on set!"

"Cloe, I hope you aren't still mad at us about yesterday," Yasmin began once they were outside, but Cloe cut her off.

"Not at all!" Cloe insisted. "A little healthy competition can't hurt a fabulous friendship like ours, right?"

"Well, no, but–" Yasmin said, but Cloe interrupted again.

"So it's fine! And may the best girl win!" Cloe flashed her friends a bright smile and strode determinedly towards Yasmin's car, not noticing the worried glances the girls were exchanging behind her back.

* * *

"There you girls are!" Melanie cried as Cloe, Jade, Sasha and Yasmin stepped into the town square, which had been completely transformed into a movie set.

"Wow, you guys have made our town look utterly magical!" Yasmin exclaimed. Everything was bright and sparkling, freshly painted and looking like the perfect all-American town.

"Are we late?" Sasha asked worriedly.

"Not yet," Melanie replied. "But one minute later and you would've been!"

"Be nice to these girls, Mel," Jake said as he hurried past. "They're my fans!"

Melanie gave him a quick salute, then turned back to the girls. "So Lexy just finished a new version of the script and I need you to get copies to the entire cast and crew. I left a distribution list and a pile of scripts for you in the office. When you're finished, come and find me and I'll have something else for you to do."

"Sounds good," Jade agreed. The girls ran to the trailer and emerged with armfuls of scripts.

"Okay, let's split the list into quarters, okay?" Sasha suggested. "I'll take Ahrens to Frank, Jade, you take Graham to Lowell, Yasmin, you take MacAdams to Retton and Cloe you take from there till the end."

"Who put you in charge?" Cloe demanded, completely dropping her fake-cheerful demeanour. "I notice you gave yourself all the good ones – the star, the director and the producer. That doesn't exactly seem fair."

"Do you really want to argue over the alphabet now?" Sasha snapped. "Or do you want to get our work done?"

"Sure, yeah, whatever you say, Sasha," Cloe replied, rolling her eyes. She stomped off across the square, leaving her friends staring after her again.

"Guys, I'm sorry if I was bossy," Sasha told Jade and Yasmin. "I just thought it was the fastest way to get this done, you know?"

"We know, Sasha," Jade assured her, putting her arm around her friend. "And Cloe would know it too, if she weren't so worked up about this part."

"Should we go after her?" Yasmin asked.

"We'd better get our work done first," Sasha pointed out. "We'll have time to calm Cloe down later."

But the girls were so busy running errands that they barely saw each other for the rest of the day. They gathered around Katie's food table for lunch, but Cloe wasn't there.

"Have you seen Cloe?" Jade asked Katie.

"She just stopped by to pick up lunch for that actor – what's his name? Devin something?" Cloe's mum replied.

"Devin DeVivo?" Yasmin asked.

"That's the one!" Katie agreed.

The girls grabbed sandwiches and bottles of water and settled into a shady spot at the edge of the square.

"Why would Cloe be getting Devin's lunch for him?" Yasmin wondered.

"Well, you saw how she was looking at him yesterday," Jade pointed out. "She's obviously got a crush on him. Maybe she's just trying to get his attention."

"I don't think that's all she's doing," Sasha insisted. "I think she figures if she's already hanging around with the star, it'll be easier to snag

©MGA

the co-starring gig."

"So let's go and find out," Jade suggested.

The girls finished their sandwiches, then hurried over to the biggest, nicest trailer on the set, with a star on the door reading "Devin".

"Do you think this is the one?" Jade joked.

Yasmin knocked on the door and Cloe opened it. "Can I help you?" Cloe asked coolly.

"What are you doing in here?" Yasmin asked. "Don't you have work to do?"

"This is my work now," Cloe replied. "Devin decided he needed an assistant and he picked me."

"She's just been so helpful all day that she seemed like the perfect choice," Devin called from his dressing table, where the make-up artist was getting him ready for his next scene.

"Wow, that's big news," Sasha said. "I'm surprised you didn't rush over to tell us, Cloe."

"Yeah, well, I've been kind of busy," Cloe muttered.

"Hey, are you girls all auditioning tomorrow?" Devin leaned back in his chair, peering out at the girls. "I need a co-star and fast! We need to start shooting those scenes, like, now!"

Cloe grimaced, but then plastered on a fake smile and asked her friends, "Yes, are you all still planning to audition?"

"Of course," Jade replied.

"Your choice," Cloe hissed. "But I wouldn't hold your breath."

"Gee, thanks, Clo," Sasha snapped, backing away from the door. Cloe slammed the door shut behind her and the girls stared at each other in shock outside.

"Well, I guess that explains her mood this morning," Jade declared. "It wasn't that she wanted to make up with us – she just already had a plan to get close to Devin."

"Can you believe she wasn't even going to tell us the auditions had been scheduled?" Yasmin asked once they were outside.

"Of course she wasn't," Sasha replied. "Cloe's decided she wants this part and she'll do whatever it takes to get it. But four can play at that game. Come on, girls – we have work to do."

Chapter Four

"Look, Cloe's got the attention of one of the most important people on set and I think the only way we can compete is by doing the same," Sasha told her friends as they stapled the schedules for the next morning in the production office.

"How are we going to do that?" Yasmin asked.

"We'll just follow Cloe's lead," Sasha explained. "I'm sure Lexy, Ian and Jake could all use assistants of their own. Let's prove to them that we're indispensable. Then when we show up at auditions, they'll all be rooting for us."

"But then none of us will have an advantage," Jade pointed out.

"Exactly," Sasha replied. "We'll just be levelling the playing field."

"That seems fair," Yasmin agreed. "I'll take Lexy."

"I'll work with Jake," Jade chimed in.

"And I'll go for Ian," Sasha added. "He's a tough cookie, but I think I can handle him."

"If anyone can, you can!" Yasmin exclaimed.

"Okay, then," Jade announced, "It's time to put this plan into action."

The girls fanned out to find their targets. Yasmin spotted Lexy going over the script with the director. "Oh no, my lucky pen is out of ink!" she heard the screenwriter moan in the middle of scribbling down Jake's notes.

Yasmin saw that it was a purple pen just like hers and pulled out the three extra ones she always kept in her purse for writing emergencies. She ran over to Lexy and held out the pens. "Would these help?" she asked.

"Yasmin, you're a lifesaver!" Lexy cried. "I can't write a word without my purple pens!"

"It's not like I've said anything worth writing down," Jake complained. "My brain's totally foggy – I can't seem to explain anything right."

"No, I get what you're saying," Lexy protested, but just then, Jade approached the director carrying a steaming cup of coffee.

"It's a mocha latte – I hear it's your favourite," Jade told him.

"That is exactly what I needed right now!" Jake exclaimed. "These things always improve my focus." He looked at Yasmin and Jade appraisingly and asked,

"Hey, since you're both our heroes, would you like to sit in on our notes meeting?"

"Ooh, yeah, we could use a teen perspective to help us get the dialogue right," Lexy agreed. "Would you two mind reading through this script real fast?"

Yasmin and Jade exchanged excited looks. "We'd love to!" Jade squealed.

Meanwhile, Sasha was chasing after Ian Erickson, but he was so busy shouting orders at everyone in sight that he didn't even notice her.

"Can someone please tell me how we're behind schedule already?" he demanded. He stopped short in front of the local ice cream parlour and announced, "Okay, this set is not working. Can we get another tree over here or something?"

Several crew members scrambled to find a potted tree that they could move in front of the shop to get the look Ian wanted. But as soon as they set it up, Ian complained, "No, no, too green! Find me another one!"

The crew members immediately ran off in search of a different tree and Sasha realized that she knew exactly what she could do to help the producer.

First, she dashed back to the production office and examined the schedule. "That's why we're behind," she exclaimed. "There's no way to make it from the school to the mall in five minutes – we've tried! This schedule is totally unworkable." She quickly rearranged the shooting schedule and typed up a new version, then found Ian yelling at another group of crew members in the middle of the town square.

"I know you're incredibly busy and I'm so sorry to interrupt," Sasha began, "but I think I might have a solution to your scheduling problems. Would you mind taking a look?"

She held out the new schedule and Ian was about to snap at her too when he saw that Sasha had figured out a way for them to finish the day ahead of schedule, even though they were already running behind.

"This is pure genius," he exclaimed. He looked at Sasha for the first time. "Did you come up with this yourself?"

"Yep," she replied. "See, I redid the locations so they flowed better and that shaved off a ton of time."

"Why didn't any of my people think of this?" Ian cried.

"I've lived in Stilesville my whole life," Sasha explained. "I have to know all the best shortcuts!"

"Brilliant!" Ian declared. "Kid, you're sticking with me."

"Great!" Sasha replied. "Because I have another idea that I think you might like. I'll be right back."

Sasha hurried across the set to find Jade and spotted her in the midst of her notes meeting.

While Yasmin and Lexy huddled over the script, Jade leapt around, demonstrating shots and camera angles that she

©MGA

thought might work.

"Wow, you've got a really great eye," Jake told her. "I can definitely use some of this."

"I was hoping to borrow Jade's eyes for a moment, actually," Sasha explained. "Ian's having problems with some of the sets and I'm sure Jade can help him get the right look."

"Okay, but only if I come too," Jake replied. "I'm not letting my new assistant face Ian Erickson all alone."

"New assistant?" Sasha mouthed behind Jake's back and Jade gave her a thumbs-up.

"Lexy, it looks like you and Yasmin have everything under control here," Jake added.

"Absolutely," Lexy agreed, glancing up briefly before turning back to Yasmin. "What about this line here? Any ideas to help make it pop?"

"Looks like those two have really hit it off," Sasha said, hiding a smile.

"Lexy already doesn't know how she'd manage without Yasmin," Jake declared.

"Perfect," Sasha murmured to Jade.

When they reached the town square, Ian stood with his hands on his hips, looking disapprovingly at the set.

"I know exactly what we can do with this," Jade announced. "First, we have to fix the lighting. An ice cream shop should be light and bright so it reminds you of summertime, but from out here, it looks totally dark in there." Ian motioned to a nearby lighting guy and he scurried to set up more lights inside the shop. "Then, we need some pretty curtains in the window – I'm thinking maybe pale orange, like sherbet, with polka dots to add a fun feel." Ian gestured to a props girl and she ran off to find the appropriate fabric. "That'll give you a way more appealing shot from out here – don't you think?"

"Absolutely," Jake agreed, smiling proudly at his new protégée.

"Jade's my secret weapon," Sasha explained to Ian. "She's got a spectacular sense of style."

"I can see that," Ian agreed. "And Sasha, is it?" She nodded eagerly. "I can also see that you'd be a real asset to my team. How would you like to work for me directly?"

"Like it?" Sasha squealed. "I'd love it!" She couldn't believe that her plan had worked so quickly, and so well.

The girls' new bosses had them running around all day, but they had tons of fun getting to work for some of the people they admired most. Yasmin was immersed in the world of writing, Jade

46

learned all about directing and Sasha was busy producing like crazy.

In the meantime, Cloe was stuck in Devin's trailer, listening to him complain about the life of a star while a series of hairdressers, costumers, physical trainers and agents paraded through, helping him primp, tone and plan out his career.

"I think being an actor would be totally cool," Cloe gushed.

"Yeah, could you grab me another bottle of water?" Devin asked, not listening to her.

"Oh, sure," Cloe agreed, scrambling to grab a cold bottle of water from the fridge.

"Thanks." He took a swig of water before announcing, "You know, being famous isn't as easy as everyone thinks. I mean, people expect a lot of you."

"I'm sure," Cloe interjected.

"Cloe, it's kind of hot in here," Devin said. "Is there anything you can do about that?"

"Of course, I'll turn up the air conditioning," Cloe told him. She searched for the thermostat, then fumbled with it, trying to turn it to the perfect temperature for her new boss.

"There must be some good things about it, though," Cloe insisted, sitting down across from him again. "The travel, and the fans, and the co-stars–"

"All exhausting," he interrupted. "I mean, I love my job and all, but I'm just saying it's not all fun and games."

"I totally get that," Cloe agreed. "I know all the plays I've been in have been a ton of work."

"Cloe, this is way more intense than some school play," Devin told her. "I

48

mean, I'm in practically every single scene. Do you know how many lines I have to memorize?"

"Maybe I could help you practise," Cloe suggested. "I know you have a bunch of scenes with Sophie – I bet I'd be really helpful with those."

"Oh yeah, you're trying out, aren't you?" Devin asked, choosing a shirt from a rack that Bella, the costume designer, had brought to show him. "Look, I'm kind of tired right now, but maybe we can squeeze something in tomorrow, okay?"

"No problem," Cloe replied, trying to hide her disappointment.

"Hey, it's been a long day – why don't you head home?" he suggested.

"Thanks," Cloe said.

"Oh, but first, could you find me the latest issue of Movie Scene Magazine?" he added. "They should have some copies over at the production office."

"Sure thing," Cloe told him, but when she got outside, she slumped against the side of his trailer and sighed. "Not exactly the glamorous Hollywood job I'd pictured," she muttered, before trudging off in search of yet another thing Devin absolutely had to have.

Chapter Five

"Should we try to find Cloe?" Yasmin asked. She and her friends had finished their first long day on set and they were totally ready to get home and chill for the night.

"I don't think she exactly wants to see us right now," Sasha pointed out. "She made that pretty clear."

"Yeah, but she rode over with us this morning," Yasmin said. "We can't just leave her here."

"Maybe her mum's seen her," Jade suggested. They headed back to the food table and found Katie cleaning up from a long day of feeding a big cast and crew.

"Oh, yeah, Cloe's coming home with

me," Katie told the girls. "I'm sorry, I thought she'd told you."

"Nope," Sasha replied and Katie looked at her worriedly.

"Is something going on with you girls?" Cloe's mum asked. "I know she was upset about this audition thing last night, but she seemed like she was over it this morning."

"Yeah, that's what we thought too," Yasmin agreed, "but she's been avoiding us all day."

"I'm sorry to hear that," Katie replied. "But I'm sure you girls will make up soon!"

"I hope you're right," Sasha sighed. The girls turned to go, but Katie called them back.

"Why don't you take

©MGA

some snacks for the road?" she suggested. "An apple, maybe?" She tossed a shiny red apple to each of the three girls and they thanked her. Just as they were about to leave again, Cloe appeared.

"So, how's Devin?" Jade asked her.

"Fabulous, of course," Cloe declared. "And how are things going for you guys?"

"Cloe, you'll never believe it!" Yasmin cried. "I'm working for Lexy, and Sasha's working for Ian, and Jade's working for Jake! Isn't that amazing?"

"It sure is," Cloe agreed. "But I have to tell you, I still think working with my future co-star gives me an extra edge. Nice try, though."

"Geez, Cloe, can't you just be happy for us?" Yasmin complained.

"Whatever," Cloe snapped. "Now if you'll excuse me, some of us still have work to do." With that, she joined her mum behind the food table to help her pack up.

Her friends stared at her for a moment, but Cloe refused to meet their eyes and finally they gave up.

"Do you want to stay over at my place?" Yasmin asked as they piled into her car.

"Sure," Sasha agreed. "We have to be back here at the crack of dawn anyway, so we might as well all be coming from the same place."

"My thoughts exactly," Yasmin declared.

The girls all grabbed comfy spots in Yasmin's room – Yasmin on her bed, Jade on a few fluffy floor cushions and Sasha on the couch.

"So are you guys ready for the audition tomorrow?" Jade asked.

"I guess," Yasmin replied. "But you guys? I don't know if I even want to try out anymore."

"Don't tell me Cloe's getting to you," Sasha protested, but Yasmin shook her head.

"It's not that," she explained. "It's just that I'm having such a fantastic time working with Lexy that I'm not sure I want to do anything else on this movie. Maybe Cloe's right. Maybe I belong behind the scenes."

"Yas, don't sell yourself short," Jade told her. "I mean, I'm having fun with Jake too, but I still think we should all try out."

"Totally," Sasha agreed. "Working with Ian is awesome, but not cool enough to make me turn down a starring role in his movie!"

"I guess you've got a point," Yasmin admitted. "I mean, it would be fun to be a movie star."

"Of course it would!" Jade cried. "You'd get to wear gorgeous outfits and try out fabulous new hairstyles and make-up looks, and get paid for it! What's not to love?"

"Well, I'm convinced," Sasha announced. "So let's get some practising done."

"Do you guys know which scenes we're supposed to work on?" Yasmin wanted to know.

"Jake said we could pick any scene between Devin and Sophie," Jade replied. "So I was thinking we should all choose different ones."

"Maybe we should call Cloe," Yasmin suggested. "That way we could coordinate which scenes we choose with her, too."

"Yas, did you forget that Cloe's barely

speaking to us?" Sasha asked. "There's no way she'll want to rehearse with us."

"Guys, she's our best friend," Yasmin insisted. "Don't you think we have to at least try?"

"Yasmin's right," Jade admitted.

Yasmin grabbed the cordless phone from her bedside table and speed-dialled Cloe.

"Hello?" Cloe answered.

"Cloe, it's Yasmin. We're all hanging out at my place and we wanted to see if you'd like to join us." Yasmin slumped back on her bed, nervously awaiting her friend's answer.

"Oh, I don't know, I have to be back at the set really early tomorrow," Cloe said in a rush.

"Us too," Yasmin told her. "We're heading to bed soon, but we wanted to run through a few scenes for the audition first."

"Wait, how do you know which scenes to practise?" Cloe demanded.

"Well, you know Jade's working with the director," Yasmin explained, "And he told her we could pick our own scenes. As long as Devin's in them, of course."

"Why would anyone pick a scene without Devin? Isn't being in a scene with him the whole point of getting that part?" Cloe joked, but then seemed to remember that she was mad at her friend. "I mean, yeah, that's what Devin told me too."

"Oh, good," Yasmin replied. "So, do you want to come over to rehearse with us?"

Cloe paused and Yasmin looked at her friends excitedly, sure she was going to say yes, but finally Cloe murmured, "I don't think that's really a good idea."

"You can't stay mad at us forever, Cloe," Yasmin told her.

"I'm not mad at you, Yas, I swear," Cloe said. "Look, I've gotta go. I'll see you tomorrow, okay?" Before Yasmin could say anything else, Cloe hung up, leaving Yasmin listening to the dial tone.

"Let me guess," Sasha began, "She said no."

"Hey, at least you tried," Jade interjected, jumping onto the bed beside Yasmin and putting her arm around her friend.

"The weird thing was, it didn't sound like Devin had told her she should pick her own scene," Yasmin said. "They seemed all buddy-buddy this afternoon, but I don't think things are going so well any more."

"Why?" Sasha asked. "What'd she say?"

"It wasn't what she said," Yasmin explained. "It's what she didn't say. She wasn't gloating about her new job any more and she sounded, well – she sounded totally fed up."

"Maybe working for her crush isn't as much fun as she thought it would be," Jade suggested.

"That would be awkward," Yasmin agreed. "I just wish she would tell us what's going on so we could help."

Back in Cloe's room, she was wishing exactly the

©MGA

same thing. "My friends all have fabulous jobs and mine couldn't be more boring," she moaned, burrowing under her covers with her puppy, Cashmere, by her side. "And I was so mean to them that there's no way I can go running back to them now!" she told the dog.

The brown and cream-coloured puppy licked her face energetically and Cloe finally smiled. "Well, at least I have you to cheer me up, right, Cashmere?" But her puppy couldn't answer and Cloe found herself wishing she'd accepted Yasmin's invitation after all.

Chapter Six

When Yasmin, Jade and Sasha stepped outside the next day, they found Cloe waiting for them on the porch with their favourite smoothies in hand.

"Anyone need a pick-me-up?" Cloe asked, smiling shyly at her friends.

"I never turn down a smoothie," Jade replied. Cloe handed her a strawberry smoothie. Jade took a long sip and smiled. "Mmm, that almost makes being up at seven a.m. feel worthwhile."

"Can I come in for a minute?" Cloe passed smoothies to Yasmin and Sasha, looking from one friend to the next, her blue eyes wide with hope.

"We kind of need to get over to the

set," Sasha told her.

"But you can come with us, if you want," Yasmin added. "There's room for one more."

"That'll work," Cloe agreed. The girls hopped into Yasmin's car and Cloe took a deep breath. "I feel terrible about the way I've been acting and I know a few smoothies can't make it up to you, but it's a start, right?"

"Yeah, it's a start," Jade said.

"So what brought about this sudden change of heart?" Sasha wanted to know. "You seemed pretty set on not speaking to us yesterday."

"It's just that I wanted this part so much and I felt like you guys didn't even care," Cloe explained. "But now I don't know if I even want it at all."

"What are you talking about?" Yasmin cried. "You'd be amazing in that role!"

"Thanks, Yas," Cloe replied, "but after yesterday, let's just say I don't think Devin and I have the right chemistry."

"Wait, what happened?" Jade asked, leaning forward from the back seat.

"It's just, he's really self-absorbed and demanding, and he didn't want to listen to anything I had to say," Cloe complained.

"Wait, you're telling us that movie stars are self-centred?" Yasmin teased. "I don't believe it!"

"I know, I know, I should have seen it coming," Cloe sighed. "And I should have worked together with you guys instead of going behind your backs. I just – I thought working for him was the only way I could get this part. So I went for it."

"I still think it was a good move, Clo," Sasha told her. "I mean, that's how we got the idea to work for our own role models and that's been going great."

"Glad I could help," Cloe murmured. "Too bad my big plan has been a total disaster for me!"

"It can't be that bad," Yasmin said. "Come on, tell us what happened."

"Well, I wanted to practise lines with him, but he kept telling me to run boring errands," Cloe complained.

"Um, Cloe, that is kind of what an assistant does," Sasha pointed out.

"I know, it's just that I thought he would be different, you know?" Cloe moaned. "He seemed so nice and down-to-earth when we met him. I just figured we'd hit it off right away."

"Cloe, it'll be okay," Yasmin declared. "You'll get that part and then you won't have to work for Devin any more."

"But I'd still have to work with him,"

Cloe cried.

"I suspect he's a little nicer to his co-stars than he is to his assistants," Jade told her.

"I guess that's true," Cloe admitted. "But it doesn't matter, because I'm not going to get the part. I felt so bad about our fight that I couldn't practise at all last night."

"You're a fantastic actress," Yasmin assured her. "I'm sure you'll do great."

"Maybe, but so will you girls," Cloe sighed. "And you've all been practising together, so you're way ahead of me. I'm totally doomed!"

Yasmin pulled into a parking space outside the mall, then turned to look worriedly at her best friend in the passenger seat.

"You are not doomed," Sasha announced. "Look, we don't have to be on set for half an hour. We'll practise in the car until it's time to go and then we can practise some more at lunchtime. I promise we'll have you ready in time."

Cloe looked up at her friends and smiled. "You three are the greatest!"

"Yeah, yeah, we know," Jade joked, pulling her script out of her messenger bag. "Now come on – we've got a lot of work to do!"

*   *   *

By the time she strode onto the set with her three best friends, Cloe was actually feeling good about her audition. But her smile disappeared when she spotted Devin waiting for her, his arms crossed over his chest.

"Cloe, I thought I asked you to bring me an egg-white omelette for breakfast this morning," Devin called, sounding annoyed.

"I asked my mum to make you one at the food table," Cloe explained. "Someone on her staff was supposed to bring it to you."

"Yeah, I got it, but I asked you to bring my breakfast," Devin snapped. "And that didn't happen, now did it?"

"Why does it matter who brought it?" Cloe asked.

"Because I don't like being bothered by random people first thing in the morning and I don't like having my specific requests completely ignored," he shouted.

"Guess I've got my work cut out for me," Cloe whispered to her friends. "Hope your days are better than mine."

The girls shot her sympathetic looks as she headed over to Devin. "Was the omelette okay, though?" they heard her ask. "I gave them careful instructions on how you wanted it."

"It was good," he admitted as she followed him toward his trailer. "I'm sorry I flipped out. It just really throws off my acting when things don't go as planned. And I have a big day today, so I have to be on top of my game. Did you know they're holding auditions for my co-star today?"

"I did hear something about that," Cloe told him. She couldn't believe he'd completely forgotten that she was auditioning for that part herself.

Meanwhile, Yasmin found Lexy sitting under a tree, reading through the latest version of her script.

"Hey there!" Lexy called when she saw

Yasmin. "Are you ready for your big audition today?"

"I've read the script so many times that I could probably recite the whole thing," Yasmin replied. "So that's gotta help, right?"

"Definitely!" Lexy agreed. "But would you mind reading it one more time? It still feels to me like something's missing."

"No problem." Yasmin sat cross-legged beside the screenwriter and started reading.

Nearby, Jade was helping Jake set up his first shot of the day. "This is my favourite view of the mall," she announced. "See, you get the trees in the background and the flower beds out front – doesn't it look amazing?"

"Yeah…" Jake began slowly.

"Of course you should do whatever you think works," Jade said hurriedly.

"You're the directing genius!"

"No, it totally works," Jake told her. "I'm just blown away that you have a favourite view of the mall!"

"Doesn't everyone?" Jade asked with a grin.

Just then, Sasha was heading into the mayor's office with Ian. "Do you really think you can help us get clearance to shoot in the school?" the producer asked her.

"Absolutely," she declared. "Mayor Davis and I are tight."

"Sasha, how good to see you," the mayor called from behind her desk. "Please, come right in."

Ian and Sasha took seats across from her and Ian explained, "We're very much enjoying shooting in your town and we'd like to make use of the high school as well."

"You know school starts in a few weeks," Mayor Davis replied. "We can't have your crew interfering with that."

"Of course not," Ian agreed. "We're planning to shoot everything in the next two weeks and if we need to do any additional shots, we'll do them before or after school hours."

"That sounds doable to me," the mayor replied. "And if Sasha's vouching for you, I don't have any objections."

"Mayor Davis, you're the absolute coolest!" Sasha cried, leaping out of her seat. Catching herself, she sat back down and said, "I mean, thank you so much for your help."

But Mayor Davis just laughed. "Hey, I don't mind being called the coolest. Maybe I can get that added to my nameplate." She gestured towards the plaque on her door.

"I'll have one of our crew members make up a new plaque right away," Ian told her, totally serious. By the end of the day, he had a "Mayor Davis, The Absolute Coolest," plaque delivered to her door, which would remain propped on her desk for the rest of her time in office.

As they headed back to the set, Ian announced, "We make a great team, you and me."

"We do, don't we?" Sasha agreed, thrilled that her producing career was off to such a spectacular start.

Chapter Seven

The girls met up again at lunch to practise and by the time the auditions rolled around that afternoon, they were all super-excited. Production stopped so that Jake, Ian and Lexy, along with the casting director, Jordan Lowell, could all sit in on auditions.

Cloe, Jade, Sasha and Yasmin met up on the front steps of their high school and headed for the classroom where auditions were being held.

"It feels weird being here during the summer," Cloe murmured.

"Especially since they've transformed it into a totally different school for the movie," Jade pointed out.

Since Ian and Sasha's meeting that morning, the whole crew had been scrambling to turn Stilesville High into Viewpoint High School, where the movie was set. The blue and gold Stilesville High banner over the front doors had been replaced with a green and white Viewpoint sign and flyers for nonexistent Viewpoint activities hung from all the notice boards in the halls.

Everything that would show up in the movie had been freshly painted, so all the

©MGA

lockers were bright and shiny and the school-year dings had been wiped away from all the walls.

"It's a new and improved Stilesville High," Sasha added. "Not too bad for one day's work!"

By the time the girls reached the drama classroom, it was already crowded with actresses hoping to snag the part. They spotted their friends Meygan and Felicia sitting together in a corner of the room and waved, then pushed their way through the jam-packed room to say hello.

"I didn't know you girls were trying out!" Cloe exclaimed when they reached Meygan and Felicia.

"Well, we've been seeing flyers about it all over town and we thought it would be fun to give it a try," Felicia explained. "But where have you girls been lately? No one's seen you all week!"

"We've been working on this movie, actually," Sasha told her. "And it's been amazing!"

"You guys are so smart," Meygan sighed. "I don't know why I didn't think of getting a job on the set."

"Yeah, well, it's not as much fun as you might think," Cloe complained and her friends patted her on the back comfortingly.

Jake, Ian, Lexy and Jordan filed in from behind the small stage at the front of the room and took seats facing it. Everyone started to quieten down and Jordan's assistant, Owen, began passing out numbers to everyone in the crowd.

"If you've had a chance to read the whole script, you can pick your own scene," Owen shouted above the remaining chatter. "Otherwise, there are copies of the prom scene on a table by the door – feel free to pick one up if you need it."

A group of girls swarmed around the table and grabbed copies of the scene.

"Catch you girls later!" Felicia called as she and Meygan rushed over to get copies of their own.

"Wow, I'm glad we aren't just getting our scenes right now," Yasmin whispered to her friends.

"Yeah, I'd say working on set is giving us that extra edge we were hoping for!" Jade declared.

But when Owen reached the girls with their numbers, they were disappointed to see that they were going last.

"If we hadn't been helping out till the last minute, we would've been first in line," Cloe complained.

"It's okay – this way we can leave them with an awesome impression," Sasha assured her, "because our auditions will be freshest in their minds."

"That's true," Cloe admitted. "But that means we'll have to sit through everyone else's auditions first."

"Not necessarily," Jade replied. "Why don't we get in some more practising out in the hall, since we have so much time?"

"Good idea," Cloe agreed, following her friends back into the hall. They sat in a row along the wall and started running through the four different scenes they'd picked, taking turns playing Sophie and Devin's character, Zach. Dejected-looking girls filed past them periodically, but the four best friends were too intent on their rehearsal to pay much attention to them.

"We're really good," Jade told her friends. "I think they should cast all of us."

"I've been working on rewrites with Lexy and there just might be some new roles cropping up," Yasmin announced.

"What?" Cloe cried. "Why didn't you tell us?"

"Because nothing's definite yet," Yasmin explained. "But believe me, I've been pushing for more girls in this movie!"

Felicia and Meygan walked out of the room and Meygan asked, "Hey, what are you guys doing out here?"

"Just sneaking in some more rehearsal time," Sasha told them. "So, how'd it go in there?"

"Tough crowd," Felicia replied. "But hey, it was fun sharing the stage with Devin DeVivo!"

"I'm sure it'll go better for you guys," Meygan added. She and Felicia waved goodbye and headed down the hallway.

"Well, that was encouraging," Yasmin sighed.

"You'll be fine," Jade insisted. "We all will."

Sasha glanced at her watch. "Whoa, we better get back in there. We've been out here for almost two hours!"

They slipped back into the drama room and were surprised to see how much it had cleared out.

They watched a few auditions and noticed that Devin seemed totally bored. Then a familiar-looking black-haired girl joined him on the small stage at the front of the room and the four friends stared at her in surprise.

"Hey, isn't that Melanie?" Jade whispered.

"It sure is," Yasmin whispered back. "I didn't know she was into acting."

"Okay, Melanie, that was good," Jordan called from the front row. "We'll get back to you by the end of the day."

As Melanie made her way offstage, Devin asked, "Could we possibly take a break? My head's spinning from trying to romance fifty different girls in a row!"

"Sure, Devin," Jake agreed. "Everyone, let's take five."

Melanie strolled past her former production assistants and did a double take. "So, I hear you all snagged yourselves promotions."

"Yeah – hope you didn't have too much trouble replacing us," Sasha said.

"Nope, you were all totally replaceable," Melanie replied. "I see you're trying out, too."

"Sure are," Cloe agreed.

"Look, I know you think you're hot stuff

and all, but let me tell you something." Melanie leaned in close and hissed, "This role is mine. I have been paying my dues on Jake's movies for two years now and I have earned this. And I'm not letting some bratty little girls steal it away from me."

"But I thought they wanted to cast a local girl," Yasmin pointed out. "And I don't think I've seen you around Stilesville before."

"They're just saying that," Melanie informed her. "It makes them sound good to the press and it smoothes the way with local officials. But in the end, they'll cast me, you'll see."

"Well, thanks for the heads-up," Jade replied briskly.

Melanie gave the four girls a long, piercing look, then turned on her heel and stalked out of the room.

"I guess we don't have to worry about competing against each other, since Melanie's already got this role in the bag," Yasmin joked.

"No way," Cloe said seriously. "We have been through way too much to give up on this part now. I don't care which one of us gets it, but one of us is getting this role."

"That's our Cloe." Jade slung her arm around Cloe's shoulders and Sasha and Yasmin joined them in a group hug.

"Okay, we're ready for the next girl," Jordan called from the front of the room. "Number fifty-two?"

"Ooh, that's me!" Cloe gasped,

looking down at the fluorescent yellow number Owen had handed her earlier.

"Break a leg!" Sasha cried.

"We'll be rooting for you!" Jade added.

"You'll do great!" Yasmin chimed in.

Cloe scurried towards the stage, buoyed up by her friends' words of encouragement. But when she faced Devin on the stage, she suddenly felt her confidence drain away.

"Cloe! There you are!" Devin exclaimed. "I've been looking for you all afternoon."

"I've been here, waiting to audition," she explained.

"Huh," he said. "I didn't know you were auditioning."

Cloe wanted to remind him that they had talked about it several times, but she figured it wasn't worth it. Instead, she took a deep breath and gave him her most dazzling smile. "Well, here I am!"

"Cloe, which scene will you be doing?" Jake asked.

"The birthday party scene," she replied. "Devin, are you ready?"

"Sure," he said, looking bored again. But as soon as Cloe started her lines, he perked right up. She knew them all by heart and she really made her character come to life.

When they finished the scene, Cloe's friends burst into applause at the back of the room. "Cloe, that was amazing," Devin told her. "I had no idea you were such a talented actress."

Cloe looked away, blushing. "That means a lot, coming from you."

"I mean it," he insisted. "And I'm sorry I've been so hard on you. I thought you'd have to work your way up as an assistant, but look at you! You're already a star."

"Well, we'll see what they have to say about that," Cloe replied, gesturing to the director, producer, writer and casting director in the front row. They were all leaning in towards each other, whispering rapidly about Cloe's audition.

"I think they liked you too," Devin murmured.

"Thank you very much," Jordan said after another moment. "Sorry to rush you, but we need to move on to the next scene."

Cloe dashed offstage and hugged her friends, trying to contain her excitement. "I know nothing's final yet, but it just felt so good to have such an awesome audition!"

"You were really fantastic," Sasha told her.

"Number fifty-three?" Jordan called.

"That's me!" Sasha declared.

"Now you get up there and do an amazing job too!" Cloe cried.

Sasha performed a scene set at a pre-match rally and everyone seemed to love her too. Then Jade did a spectacular job with a classroom scene and Yasmin finished up with a fabulous rendition of Sophie and Zach's first date.

"Well, I think that's it for the day," Jordan announced once Yasmin had left the stage. "And let me just say that you girls have made this decision very difficult for us! Thank you all for coming. I'll announce our decisions in one hour."

"Wow, that's fast!" Sasha exclaimed.

"I'm glad," Yasmin told her. "I can't wait for these auditions to be over so things can just get back to normal between us."

"That's right," Jade agreed. "Then we can go back to our nice, normal jobs helping out on an amazing Hollywood movie!"

Chapter Eight

The girls kept themselves busy around the set for the next hour, but they all kept looking at their watches, too anxious to find out who'd got the part to pay much attention to their work.

"It's time," Sasha announced finally and the girls ran back to the front steps of the school, where Jordan was planning to make the announcement.

"It wasn't an easy choice, but we've decided to cast Cloe as our Sophie Grace," Jordan declared. Cloe's friends all cheered for her, while the other actresses wandered off, looking disappointed.

"What?" Melanie shrieked. "I'm supposed to be Sophie! I'm perfect for that part!"

"I'm sorry, Melanie, but Cloe had a better audition," Jordan explained. "Maybe next time, okay?"

Melanie whirled to face Cloe and her three best friends, her grey eyes glinting with fury. "You girls think you can just stroll onto a movie set and have everything go your way, don't you? Well let me just tell you, you've got another thing coming." She stalked off, leaving the girls staring after her.

"She didn't take that well, did she?" Jade asked.

"Not at all," Cloe agreed. "But how are you guys taking it? I know I was kind of a jerk about it before, but I really didn't want to steal the part away from any of you."

"Cloe, you earned that part," Sasha told her, "so of course we're happy for you. Just like you would've been happy for any of us if we'd got it."

"I really would have," Cloe declared. "And I couldn't have done it without you! You're the best friends ever."

"So you'll remember us when you're famous?" Jade teased.

"Absolutely!" Cloe exclaimed.

The girls were jumping up and down with excitement when Devin strolled over. "I just heard the news. Congratulations, Cloe – you deserve it."

"I'm really looking forward to working with you," Cloe told him.

Devin looked down at his feet, embarrassed. "I just hope our previous working relationship won't, you know, impact our new co-star status."

"Don't worry about it," Cloe replied. "I know I can learn a lot from you. I'm just glad this time it'll be about acting, instead of omelettes."

Devin laughed and the girls all joined in. "I was an awful boss, wasn't I?" he asked.

"I've had worse," Cloe assured him.

"Well, I'll be way better as a co-star, I promise," he declared.

"There's my new leading lady!" Jake called, walking up to the group clustered just outside the high school, with Ian and Lexy at his side. "Cloe, I need you in rehearsals right now. We need to start shooting your scenes by the end of the week, so we've got a lot of work to do!"

Then Jake pulled Jade aside and murmured, "I know you wanted that part, but you've been so much help with my directing that I just couldn't give you up. I hope you don't mind."

"Not at all," Jade told him. "It's been

awesome helping you out and honestly I'd rather keep doing that than act in this movie anyway."

"I'm so happy to hear you say that," Jake told her, "because I want to make you my new assistant director. It's a lot more work, but I think you're definitely up to it. What do you say?"

"I'd love to!" Jade squealed.

"Great," Jake said. "Then you can help me direct Cloe in her first scene. Something tells me you might know how to get a great performance out of her."

"I think I could manage that," Jade agreed.

"And Sasha?" Ian added, stepping forward. "Besides myself, you are the most organized person I've ever met. Would you like to be my co-producer?"

"Would I ever!" Sasha exclaimed.

Lexy chimed in, "Yasmin, I need help with another rewrite."

"Okay, Lexy," Yasmin agreed, trying to hide her disappointment at being handed more work instead of a promotion like her friends. Turning to the girls, she added, "Congratulations, you guys."

"I think congratulations are in order for you, too," Lexy told her. "After all the help you've given me on this script, I want you to have a writing credit on this movie. It'll say 'Written by Lexy and Yasmin' up there on the big screen!"

"Oh my gosh!" Yasmin

cried, jumping up and down with excitement. "Are you serious?"

"Absolutely," Lexy replied. "If you can help me get this script in shape tonight."

"Not a problem," Yasmin declared. "We'll order pizza and stay up all night if we have to!"

"That's the spirit," Lexy said, laughing. So while the others headed off to rehearsals, Yasmin sat down in Lexy's trailer with her, ready to whip up a fresh take on the script.

"You know what this script could really use?" Yasmin asked. Lexy looked up from her copy of the script expectantly and Yasmin continued, "Some friends for Sophie! I mean, right now it's totally focused on Zach and his buddies, but it's supposed to be a story about both of them, right?"

"That's true," Lexy admitted. "But if I

add more characters this late in the game, how are we ever going to get them cast fast enough?"

"We can worry about that later," Yasmin replied. "Look, we have to do what's best for the script, right?" Lexy nodded and Yasmin hurried on. "So let's try giving Sophie a few gal-pals and see how it works, okay?"

"I guess it's worth a try," Lexy agreed. "But where would you want to add them in?"

"Well, definitely at the football game," Yasmin began. "I mean, Sophie can't be sitting all alone when Zach comes up to talk to her for the first time. And the prom's way more fun if you go in a group, so I'm sure Sophie would want to double-date with her friends."

"See, this is what I love about having a teenage co-writer!" Lexy cried. "I hardly even remember my prom!"

"Come on, Lexy, you aren't that much older than I am," Yasmin told her.

"That's very sweet of you to say," Lexy replied, laughing. "But seriously, I am."

"Well, you've got the world of high school all figured out," Yasmin declared. "This could totally be about life at Stilesville High – once we add in some awesome girlfriends, that is."

"Okay, okay, we're writing them in." Lexy picked up a fresh purple pen and started scribbling on the first page of the football game scene. Then she flipped a few pages ahead and asked, "Wait, shouldn't they be in the lunch room with her too?"

"Totally!" Yasmin exclaimed. "See, now you're thinking like a high school girl!"

Chapter Nine

The next morning, Cloe started shooting her very first movie scenes. First she got a complete makeover, then the costume designer dressed her up in a totally cute outfit – it was even more fun than she had imagined it would be! But once the cameras started rolling, Cloe started having a little trouble thinking like Sophie instead of just being herself.

"Okay, remember, Sophie likes chemistry class," Jade called to her friend. "So try to sound excited when you're explaining this lab work to Zach, okay?"

Cloe nodded, and Jake added, "Okay, let's take two."

"Zach, you can totally do this!" Cloe cried, reciting her character's lines. "Look, you just pour this test tube into this beaker," she explained, leaning over her co-star, "and voila!"

A loud bang echoed through the classroom and Cloe jumped back from the lab table as a puff of smoke engulfed both Devin and her. "Was that supposed to happen?" she cried.

"No," Jade replied. "I think someone must've switched the chemicals."

"But no one's been in here, except the

©MGA

100

crew," Jake pointed out.

"Well then, maybe someone just put out the wrong ingredients," Jade suggested. "Chemistry can be pretty confusing, if you aren't used to it."

She darted over to the cabinets that held all the chemicals to be used for classroom experiments and added, "Luckily, I am!" She quickly examined labels, pushing various bottles aside, then triumphantly held up the two vials she was looking for. "These will do the trick!" She cleared away the still-smoking beaker and set up the new chemicals. "Does that look right?" Jade asked the director, once she had rearranged everything on the table.

"It looks perfect," Jake agreed. "I didn't know I was getting a science whiz as well as a visual genius!"

"Yeah, well, I'm multi-talented," Jade

replied with a grin.

"Okay, let's try this again," Jake announced.

Cloe repeated her lines and this time, green sparks burst out of the top of the beaker as Devin, playing Zach, looked into Cloe-as-Sophie's eyes. "Amazing," he murmured.

"And, cut!" Jake shouted. "That was great. I think we got it. Jade?"

"I totally believed that Cloe was into chemistry," Jade replied. "Now that's some impressive acting!"

"Jade!" Cloe complained, but she couldn't help giggling.

"Okay, on to scene seven," Jake announced and the crew hurried to pack up their equipment and move to their next set. Cloe met the costume and make-up crew in the girls' bathroom for a quick change into chic black pants and a sparkly tube top for Zach and Sophie's first-date scene. The hairdresser set Cloe's hair in soft waves as the make-up artist brushed on smoky eye shadow.

Bella, the costume designer, stepped back to look at Cloe, then called, "Accessories!" One of her assistants rushed forward holding a long golden necklace.

"There!" Bella declared after she had arranged the necklace in three long loops around Cloe's neck. "Now you look ready to go and win Devin's heart." Her green eyes sparkling, the costume designer corrected herself, "I mean, Sophie looks ready to romance Devin."

Cloe blushed, but all she could manage to say was a soft "Thank you!" before she hurried off to her next scene.

"Wow, you guys really glammed this place up!" Cloe exclaimed as she stepped into the restaurant where the date scene was set. Their favourite neighbourhood Italian place, Gigio's, had been transformed into an elegant eatery, with white tablecloths and flickering candles on every table and a tuxedo-clad maitre d' waiting at the door.

"They totally glammed you up, too!" Jade declared. "You totally look like a star."

"That's the magic of movies!" Cloe replied.

"Cloe, over here!" Devin called. He was sitting at a table in the middle of the room, surrounded by extras pretending to be at dinner too. His face lit up when Cloe approached, but all he said was, "Are you ready?"

"I was working on these lines all night," she told him. "This scene is the one I wanted to make sure I got right."

Devin smiled and Jake announced that they were ready to start.

"You didn't have to do all this for me," Cloe said, reciting her lines.

"Yes, I did," Devin replied as Zach, looking at her meaningfully.

Cloe took a sip of her water, pretending to be flustered by his gaze, and immediately spat it out. "Ugh!" she cried.

"Cut!" Jake cried. "Well, that kind of ruined the mood."

"It's salt water!" Cloe declared.

Jade and Jake exchanged a glance. "Did someone switch the props in here, too?" Jake demanded. No one answered and he called, "Well, come on, let's get her some nice, fresh water this time!" Two young crew members scurried to bring fresh water glasses for both Cloe and

105

Devin and then Jake started the scene again.

"I have to say, this is a pretty good first date," Cloe said later in the scene.

"I was hoping you'd say that." Devin leaned forward. "Because I have something to ask you." Cloe looked up at him hopefully and he continued, "Sophie, would you be my date for the prom?"

"I thought you'd never ask!" she squealed.

"I think we got it!" Jake announced.

As everyone headed for the next set, Devin fell into step beside Cloe. "You know, I wasn't totally acting in there."

"Wha – what do you mean?" Cloe stammered, stumbling over her words in her excitement.

"I think we have a real spark," Devin told her. "Don't you?"

"I might have noticed something," Cloe replied coyly.

"Maybe we could grab dinner sometime," he suggested. "Not as Sophie and Zach, but you know, just as ourselves."

"I think that could be arranged," Cloe agreed, a smile spreading across her face. She couldn't believe her movie-star crush had just asked her out on a real date and she couldn't wait to tell her friends!

"I'll see you at the mall, okay?" she asked, then hurried off to find Jade.

"Let me guess," Jade said when she saw the look on Cloe's face. "Devin asked you out."

"How'd you know?" Cloe cried.

"Hey, I saw the scene in there," Jade explained. "It obviously wasn't all acting."

The girls both giggled as they stepped

into the mall and then stopped short, stunned to see how huge it looked now that it was completely empty.

"Whoa – a whole mall, just for us!" Jade cried. "This is like a dream come true!"

"Remember, we're here to work," Sasha called, walking up with Ian. "We cleared out the mall for two hours and we have a flock of extras waiting to set the scene, so we've got to get started."

"Why not just film the mall with all the regular people walking around?" Cloe wanted to know. "Wouldn't that be easier?"

"Not at all," Ian explained. "Most people get so excited when they see a camera, there's no telling what they'll do. But all of our extras are carefully chosen and prepped for the scene, so they know exactly how to handle themselves."

"Places, everyone!" Jake shouted. Cloe stepped into Etc., one of her favourite stores, and found a bunch of extras waiting for her in there, pretending to shop. Bella helped her change in the fitting room and after a quick redo of her make-up, Cloe stepped out of the shop, a bunch of prop shopping bags dangling from her arm, and spotted Devin walking by.

"Oh!" she gasped and ducked back into the store. And then she felt someone shove her from behind and found herself sprawled across the gleaming tiles of the mall's main corridor.

"Zach, how nice to see you!" called a high-pitched voice. Cloe saw a pair of long legs step over her and saunter over towards Devin.

"Cut! Cut!" Jake yelled. "Melanie, what on earth are you doing?"

Cloe sat up slowly, rubbing at her head and looked up to see Melanie glaring back at Jake with her hands on her hips. The production coordinator looked totally glamorous, in a black mini-skirt and red sleeveless top, her glossy black hair carefully curled under at the ends and her lips a shiny, cherry red. But she also looked a little crazed.

"I'm just trying to save the scene," Melanie announced.

"Cloe, are you okay?" Jade asked, as she and Sasha rushed over to help their friend up.

"I think so," Cloe replied. She smoothed out her shirt and added, "I just hope the fall didn't ruin my outfit!"

"Yeah, she's fine," Sasha said, grinning.

"Are you sure you aren't hurt?" Devin cried, running over.

"No worries," Cloe assured him. "I can

handle a few spills."

"You guys know how hard I've worked on your last three movies," Melanie shouted, stalking towards Jake and Ian. The girls and Devin turned to watch the off-screen drama unfolding in the middle of the set. "But every time I go for something a little more exciting than production coordinator, you totally ignore me. And then these girls just waltz in here and you give every single one of them amazing jobs. It's just not fair!"

"Come on, Mel, these girls have worked hard too," Jake pointed out. "And I know you wanted the Sophie role, but Cloe was right for the part. I'm sorry, but that's the way it works."

"But she keeps messing up!" Melanie declared. "She got the chemistry experiment wrong, she spat water all over everything and now she totally wiped out in the middle of the mall! She's a disaster."

"I didn't fall," Cloe protested. "You pushed me!"

"Okay, Melanie, that's enough," Ian announced. "Security!"

A group of security guards approached from the mall entrance, where they'd been patrolling to make sure no one wandered in.

"Wait, no!" Melanie cried. "I was just trying to prove I could do the part. I didn't want anyone to get hurt. I–"

But then Lexy and Yasmin burst in through the glass doors,

waving copies of their new script excitedly.

"Don't shoot another scene till you've read this!" Yasmin exclaimed, as everyone turned to stare at the pair of screenwriters.

Chapter Ten

"This script is fantastic!" Jake declared. Shooting had stopped so everyone could read the new script, while Yasmin and Lexy anxiously watched their colleagues.

"We made sure not to change anything you've already shot," Lexy explained. "But Yasmin had this total brainstorm and we just had to work it into the movie."

"The only problem is, you've given Sophie three friends and a nemesis," Jake continued, "which totally works, but who's going to play them?"

"What if Sasha, Jade and I played Sophie's friends?" Yasmin suggested.

"They're really good at being my friends, so I'm sure they'd be awesome as

Sophie's friends, too!" Cloe chimed in.

"They did have good auditions," admitted Jordan, who had been called over to read the revised script.

"No way am I giving up my co-producer," Ian protested.

"But that's the beauty of these roles," Lexy explained. "They're important, but they're small, so the girls can play these parts and still do their other jobs."

"I'm sold!" Jake announced. "But who's going to play the nemesis?"

Cloe glanced over at Melanie, who was slumped against the wall at the edge of the set, flanked by security guards. "I think I might know just the girl."

*   *   *

"You really don't mind sharing the spotlight with us?" Yasmin asked Cloe the next day at lunch, after they'd just finished shooting their first scene all together.

"There's no one I'd rather share it with," Cloe declared.

"Besides, you're still the star!" Jade pointed out.

"Well, yeah, that doesn't hurt either," Cloe admitted, grinning.

"And we all get to keep doing the things we love best on this movie!" Yasmin added.

"Can I join you?" Melanie asked, striding up to the table where the girls were sharing the yummy sandwiches Katie had made for them. She looked nervous, but the four best friends immediately scooted over to make room for her.

"I wanted to tell you how sorry I am," Melanie began. "I wasn't trying to hurt anyone, I swear. I just wanted that part so badly that I got completely carried away."

"It's okay," Cloe assured her. "I did things I'm not proud of when I was trying to get this part, too."

"Plus we all totally owe you for giving us a chance to work on this movie in the first place," Sasha told Melanie.

"No, I owe you guys for helping me get cast in a totally cool part!" Melanie replied.

"What do you say we just call it even?" Jade suggested.

"I'd like that," Melanie agreed. She looked down at her hands, then took a deep breath and said, "Look, I know I was awful to you guys, but I was hoping that maybe, well – that we could be friends."

"Of course we can!" Yasmin cried. "Just not on set, okay?"

"Right," Melanie said. "On set, we're sworn enemies."

"But off the set, we're pals," Sasha added.

*   *   *

The next two weeks were a blur of costume changes, learning lines and camera shots. The shoot culminated with the prom scene, set in the town square, which had been decked out with twinkling lights and fluttering streamers.

The girls were dazzling too, Cloe in a sparkling black evening gown, Jade in a silvery sheath, Sasha in a glitzy white dress and Yasmin in a floor-length golden gown. Melanie was there too, looking glam in a midnight-blue dress, though of course she was in character and getting ready for a showdown with the girls.

"This is way better than our real prom," Cloe announced.

"Yeah, and our prom dates aren't bad, either," Jade added. Cloe was escorted by Devin, looking even more handsome in his tux and her friends were paired with three other cute actors who were playing Devin's pals in the movie.

The girls danced all night and were having so much fun that even though they were saying their lines, they hardly noticed the cameras were rolling.

But finally Jake announced, "That's a wrap!" and the crew immediately started tearing down all the magical-looking decorations.

"I can't believe it's all over!" Yasmin cried.

©MGA

"It's not," Sasha pointed out. "It's just the start of our awesome Hollywood careers!"

But before they could continue rising through the ranks of the movie business, the girls had to go back to school.

"I can't stop looking for cameras around every corner," Cloe declared on the first day of school. "I'm so used to this being one big set that it feels strange to be going to real classes here!"

"Yeah, well, get used to it," Sasha teased. "We've got a big year ahead of us. Now that we've conquered Hollywood, it's time to make a splash on the high school scene. Between all our activities and our new classes, we'll be even busier than we were on that movie set!"

"I don't know if I can imagine being busier than that," Yasmin sighed. "I'm still recovering!"

"But it was all worth it!" Jade reminded her and her best friends instantly agreed.

The girls found their new lockers and started personalizing them with photos, make-up bags and mirrors. But then Cloe paused, noticing that all the other students in the hallway seemed to be watching them. "Do you think everyone knows we're stars?" Cloe asked.

"They might have heard something about High School Sweethearts, set to be the biggest blockbuster of the holiday season!" Jade replied.

"And they might have heard about the awesome premiere party being held next month, right here in Stilesville," Sasha added.

"And maybe they heard that you'll be attending with teen heartthrob Devin DeVivo!" Yasmin told Cloe.

"So they really are talking about us," Cloe concluded.

"Probably," Jade agreed. "But it's all good stuff, so let 'em talk!"

"You know what I bet they haven't heard about yet?" Yasmin asked. "Our movie's hot new spin-off TV series, starring all four of us!"

"And written by Yasmin," Jade added.

"Produced by Sasha," Cloe chimed in.

"And directed by Jade!" Sasha exclaimed.

"Yeah, you're probably right," Jade said. "They probably haven't heard yet. But you can bet everyone will be talking about our

©MGA

latest adventures before long!"

The bell rang and the girls slammed their lockers shut, smiling as they headed off to start their new school year, this time not just as students, but also as real movie stars!

Read more about the Bratz in
these other awesome books!

Pixie Power
Spring Break Safari
Diamond Road Trip